Momo the Mouse-Plant

C urrently residing in a hovel near a large gathering of rocks on the edge of the Ward's farm, was a colony of mice. Among these mice lived one peculiar mouse, her name was Momo. Momo was a unique mouse. She was born with red fur, which among mice was most unusual. Her red fur made her look different than most other mice, who are nearly always brown or black. Momo's red fur made her feel self-conscious. Therefore, she tended to go off on her own and kept from socializing too often with the other mice, other than her family.

N ot only was Momo different because she was a red furred mouse, but she also loved the sunshine, which is an oddity as well. If you couldn't find Momo, she was most likely outside basking in the sun...or gone to bed early. You see, mice are nocturnal, which means they're most active at night. This is largely because it is too dangerous for them to be visible during the daytime, as many of their predators are active when the sun is out. At night, they are free to forage and collect food, so long as they are careful to avoid owls! Thus, it was quite curious that Momo had a tendency for going to bed earlier than the rest of her ilk. She preferred to get up whilst there was daylight so she could enjoy the sun.

T.D. WYER

One day Momo was out alone, as is typical, exploring the forest and she came across some delicious looking berries. "Those look wonderful!" she thought to herself. While darting over to collect some, she stumbled and rolled through the brush into some thin vines, which began wrapping themselves all around her as she fell, until she was completely covered and entangled in them!

S he was trapped! She was stuck! Fear began to creep into her mind. She didn't think she could disentangle herself from the mess of plants. "How will I ever get out of this?!" she wept. Panic set in, and she was quickly becoming hysterical. She needed to collect herself and calm down, she thought. "Maybe someone will hear me if I make enough noise," she thought. "Help!" she squeaked. "HELLLLLPPPP!" But no one came. She squeaked and squeaked until she was hoarse and no longer able to do so.

T eddy the tortoise was strolling through the woods, as is often the case on nice days such as this one. Teddy greatly enjoyed his walks in the woods. It was peaceful and quiet, and he always seemed to find something new and delicious to eat. Teddy primarily ate ground dwelling vegetation, berries, and herbs. Today was no different, but...it was. While on his walk, he smelled something strange melded with the fragrance of thimbleberries. Wanting to eat the thimbleberries anyway, he slowly meandered over to investigate the new smell.

As he approached the thimbleberry bush, he sniffed around, and the peculiar smell became even stronger. "A mouse? That certainly is unusual, and all wrapped up, how unfortunate!" he thought to himself. "Well that explains why the berries smell different." he said aloud. "Hello there little mouse, let me help you, I'm hungry anyway." Teddy said to the mouse. "No, don't eat me!" Momo cried.

She grimaced as Teddy began to chew through the plants she was wrapped in. "I don't eat mice, I'm a vegetarian, I don't intend on eating you, just the plants that are holding you there," Teddy mumbled, with a mouth full of vines. "There we are, you should be able to get free now, " said Teddy. "All better?"

"Oh, thank you so much. I was worried, I felt like I was trapped there forever!" said Momo. "You're very welcome," said Teddy. "How did you get yourself tangled so badly?" he asked. "Well...you see...I was excited at the prospect of gathering some berries, and I was quite hungry, so I ran too fast and tumbled over," she said. "By the way, my name is Momo. I'm a field mouse, and I live near the farm to the south. What's your name?" she asked. "Oh, I'm Teddy, I'm a tortoise."

"What's a tortoise? You look like a turtle, but MUCH bigger, and your feet are different," Momo thought aloud. "You are quite observant to notice the differences between my feet and that of a turtle," said Teddy, quite impressed. "Well your feet are at my eye level, so that's one of the first things I noticed. Well, other than your mouth when you were eating away my plant prison!" Momo interrupted. Teddy continued, "I'll let you know some other differences; as I was saying, I am similar to a turtle, however, turtles can go in and out of the water freely and swim fast, whereas I cannot. I do love water, but only to drink, though I do also love the rain. Mostly I stay on solid earth and eat fruits and plants. I am very slow, but I grow much bigger and live much longer than a turtle would." "That's neat!" stated Momo.

"Tortoises are fairly rare, especially if you're comparing them to turtles or mice.

Speaking of, you don't look like the other mice I've seen. Your fur seems brighter, and you're not usually out when it's so light. Say, why are you out when the sun is so high? Aren't you afraid of being eaten?" Teddy questioned. "Well I really enjoy the sunshine, and I like being on my own. I'm independent! I tend to do my foraging and exploring during the day if I can." said Momo in a very matter of fact way. Teddy thought she was quite brave. "You're an interesting mouse Momo, it's a pleasure to meet you." Teddy stated. "You're an interesting tortoise Teddy, I'm glad to have met you as well." stated Momo.

"**A**fter you have had your fill of berries, do you want to walk with me to the pond?" asked Teddy. "I've never been that deep in the forest. How far is it?" asked Momo. "Not very far, but I don't move quickly so it will take some time." said Teddy. "I don't mind, if it's not far. I say let's go!" Momo said excitedly.

T eddy and Momo arrived at the pond after some time. The pond was large and brimming with life, the sun glistened beautifully off the water. You could observe deer drinking across the bank, squirrels jumping on the branches high up in the trees, birds flapping in all directions, and various other woodland creatures enjoying themselves. "It's beautiful here! Do you visit often?" exclaimed Momo. "Yes, I come here quite often." said Teddy. "It's quiet and peaceful. I like to watch the fish swim in the pond and the deer as they come to drink."

"**A**re you ready to get going? It's getting late." said Teddy. "Yeah, you're right." agreed Momo. "Would you like a ride back to your burrow? It won't be fast, but it'll be safe." Teddy asked. "Sure, that'd be great." said Momo. Teddy nodded contentedly. "You can ride on my back, that way you can enjoy the sun while it is still awake," Teddy suggested. "Snakes and hawks usually don't bother me since they can't get through my shell, so they should leave us alone. If they don't, you can hide in my shell, and I'll snap at them!" Teddy moved his neck and made a snapping motion biting the air. "Hehe!" Momo squeaked.

"**N**ow that we're out of the forest, you'll have to guide me toward your burrow. I'm not the best with directions," said Teddy. "Of course," said Momo, "I'm excellent with directions! Well, except for left and right. I seem to mix those up from time to time…" Momo said, scratching her head puzzlingly.

And the two of them set off, in the open plains, headed toward the Ward's farm.

"That is it up ahead! Thank you for everything. Maybe we'll see each other again soon?" said Momo. "Yes, I think I would quite enjoy that. Goodbye Momo the Mouse-Plant. It was an interesting day, and I'm glad to have met you. Stay safe in the sun!" exclaimed Teddy as he lumbered off. "Mouse-Plant?" Momo thought to herself. "Oh, I get it. You're so silly Teddy." Momo let out a short laugh.

"Oh hello Momo, you're home late. Did you have a good day?" asked Momo's mother, as she arrived back in the burrow. "Yes, it was a great and exciting day, I had quite the adventure! I met a tortoise, which is like a huge slow turtle if you didn't know, and his name is Teddy. He's nice and funny too, and he took me to the large pond in the woods." said Momo. "That sounds nice dear; I'm glad you made a friend, now wash up so we can all eat together before the rest of us head out," said Momo's mother.

"**I** brought home some berries if you can use them." said Momo. "Oh, thank you, yes I'll bring them for a snack tonight." said Momo's mother.

"It smells wonderful, what's for dinner?" asked Momo. "Cheese, crackers, and some potatoes." said Momo's mother. "OH I LOVE THOSE!" Momo said, elated. "I know my little one. I thought you'd be excited," said Momo's mother with a smile.

"**O**of, I'm stuffed! That was delicious, thank you everyone." said Momo, having ate her fill.

"Enjoy your night out. I'm going to read for a while and then get some sleep." Momo said to her family. Momo then nestled into her fluffy bed, snuggled up to read her book, and began reading. *Once upon a time there was a brave little mouse who loved to explore...*

Until our next adventure!

Acknowledgement

For my wife Morgan, the real Mouse-Plant

Made in the USA
Middletown, DE
10 March 2022